This series is dedicated
to our own little bears:
Benjamin, Ethan, Tatum,
Oliver, and Luke.

Benjamin the Bear Gets a Sister

Story © 2013 by Shakespeare Stories, LLC

Requests for permission to make copies of any part of the work should be submitted online at info@mascotbooks.com or mailed to Mascot Books, 560 Herndon Parkway #120, Herndon, VA 20170.

PRT0713A

Printed in the United States

ISBN-13: 9781620863169
ISBN-10: 1620863162

www.mascotbooks.com

Benjamin the Bear
Gets a Sister

IT'S A GIRL!

Nancy Shakespeare

Illustrated by Katie Clouette

Benjamin the Bear has
lots of hair.

He loves his mommy
and he loves to share.

Mommy's having a baby.
She'll be here in May.

There's so much to do to
prepare for the day.

Ben dreams of his sister
and how life will change.

He asks his mom daily,
"Will you love me
the same?"

"Life will certainly change,
that much is true,

but I have room in my
heart to love both of you."

"Now you know when
she's born, she'll be
very small.

Until she grows bigger,
she can't play at all."

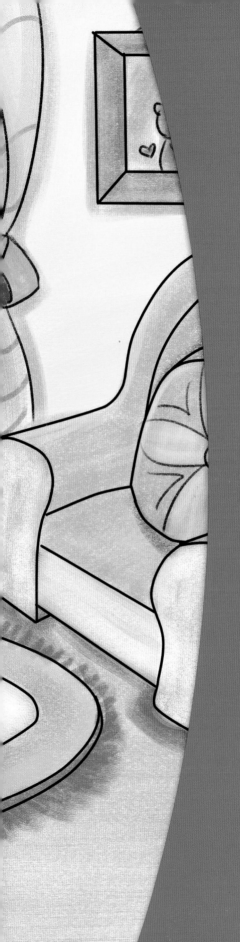

Ben hopes he can wait as
she learns how to talk.

He can help her to crawl
and teach her to walk.

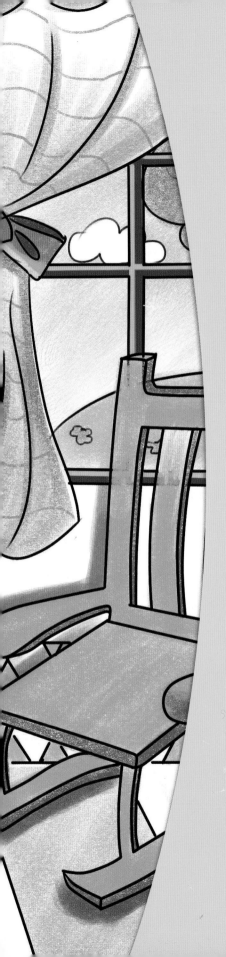

Mommy's tummy
gets bigger; his
eagerness grows.

He will teach her to
play all the games that
he knows.

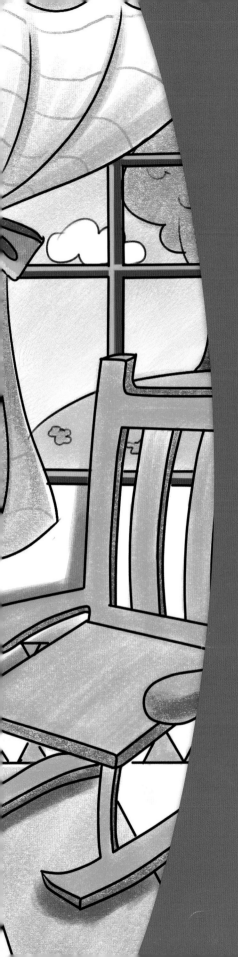

His mommy gets ready
and buys many things;

A small bed with four
sides and everything PINK!

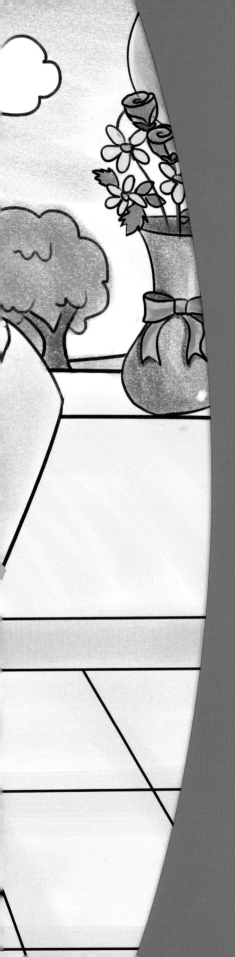

The day has arrived.
She is finally here.

She is so perfect
and little. What a
beautiful bear.

Although she looks
different than her big
brother bear,

she is Benjamin's sister.
She has just as
much hair.

Other Benjamin the Bear books:

Benjamin the Bear

Benjamin the Bear Rides on an Airplane

Benjamin the Bear Goes on a Picnic

Benjamin the Bear Goes to Kindergarten

Special Thanks

I want to thank my dear friend, Andrew Shewbart, for his guidance and expertise and for keeping me focused. Thank you also to Angel Wang and her amazing graphic design team for helping Benjamin the Bear come to life through our illustrations.

We both also want to thank our constant sources of support, our mothers, Carolyn Patterson-Franklin and Dolores Brenno-Green, our amazing husbands, Shaky and Travis, for loving us and believing in us and thank you to all our family and friends as we embark on this amazing journey.

We couldn't have done this without all of you.

Thank you so much,
Nancy & Katie

About the Author

Nancy Shakespeare has written over thirty children's short stories and is constantly coming up with new ones. Her inspiration and muse for the *Benjamin the Bear* series is her son, Benjamin. Her next series, *The Tiny Princess*, is inspired and created in her daughter, Tatum's, likeness. Also in the works is *O is for Oliver* which features the hijinks of her youngest, mischievous son, Oliver, along with other unnamed projects she and Katie are actively working on.

About the Illustrator

Katie Clouette has loved art her whole life but it wasn't until after having her two sons, Ethan and Luke, that she realized her full potential and calling as a children's book illustrator. She is incredibly gifted as an artist and knows how to create characters that are larger than life. Katie's attention to detail with all the characters is a true testament to her dedication and love for these books.